Unique Monique

Maria Rousaki

Illustrated by
Polina Papanikolaou

Kane Miller
A DIVISION OF EDC PUBLISHING

At Monique's school all the children had to wear uniforms. They were brown and blue, and Monique thought they were the ugliest colors and the ugliest clothes she had ever seen.

Every day she would tell her mother, "I don't want to wear my uniform!" Monique wanted to be different.

One day after school Monique found an old trunk in the attic.

The first thing she saw when she opened it was a huge, red hat. She tried it on, then looked at herself in the mirror. "I'm wearing this to school tomorrow," she decided.

The next morning Monique didn't complain about her uniform at all, and when she got to school everyone noticed her right away.

"Look what Monique is wearing!" called Dinos.

"It looks like a giant tomato!" Manolis shouted.

Monique was thrilled. She walked to class with her head held high, so everyone could see her hat.

"Monique, what is that thing on your head?" asked her teacher when she saw her.

"It's a red hat. Isn't it beautiful?" Monique answered.

"Remove it immediately!" her teacher demanded, and Monique had to take off her beautiful hat. (She did get to wear it during recess though, and on the way home.)

The next day everyone at school was wearing a hat!
Some were green, some were yellow, some were
small, and others were enormous.

The teachers were very upset.

"Everyone, take off your hats!" demanded the Principal.
"Hats are not allowed in school."

The only one who wasn't upset was Monique.
She had found other things in her mother's old trunk.

"Look at those glasses," said Katerina the next morning. "They're wild!"

"Those are the coolest glasses I've ever seen," Petros whispered.

Monique walked slowly to her classroom, wearing the fanciest, shiniest, most beautiful glasses in the world.

Then her teacher saw them.

"Monique, remove those glasses immediately!" she demanded.

Monique took off her glasses, but the next day… everyone was wearing glasses!

"Glasses may not be worn by children who don't need them," the Principal announced.

At home, Monique searched her mother's trunk again. She pulled out old dresses, scarves, and colorful jackets, but she couldn't find anything she could wear to school that wouldn't cover up her uniform.

Then all of a sudden she felt something down at the bottom of the trunk, something with beads. What could it be?

She pulled her hand out slowly, and when she saw what she had found she was thrilled. The perfect thing to wear to school tomorrow!

The next morning, everyone was waiting for Monique to arrive.

"Look what Monique is wearing today!" Dimitra shouted.

The other girls loved it.

And, the next day…

...all the girls had decorated barrettes and headbands in their hair. Some wore braids. Some pulled their hair to the right. Some pulled their hair to left, some to the back, some to the front, and some had pulled it into their eyes.

But their teachers decided the girls should all wear their hair neatly, out of their eyes, and that they shouldn't concern themselves with barrettes or other hair accessories.

Monique wouldn't give up. She kept trying to find ways to be different.

She started carrying a big, fancy bag to school. Then she painted her fingernails. She even wore fancy socks.

She tried lots of different things, but all of them were banned by the Principal.

Then, one day, Monique went to school looking … ordinary. She was wearing her uniform and her hair was neatly combed. She wasn't wearing a hat, and she wasn't wearing glasses or carrying a fancy bag.

Her teacher was impressed.

"Well done, Monique! It's wonderful to see you dressed properly, without breaking any school rules. Since you look so nice, why don't you come to the front, and tell us about the story we read for homework."

Monique walked slowly to the front of the class.

Monique opened her mouth to speak. Everyone stared. Monique looked very, very different.

She had the brightest and most colorful braces anyone had ever seen!

She smiled her biggest smile as she told the class about her homework.

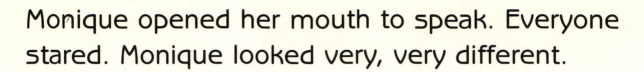

At last, she was unique.
Unique Monique!